Teddy Bear
Tears

written by **JIM AYLESWORTH**

illustrated by **JO ELLEN MCALLISTER-STAMMEN**

ATHENEUM BOOKS FOR YOUNG READERS

Atheneum Books for Young Readers
An imprint of Simon & Schuster Children's Publishing Division
1230 Avenue of the Americas
New York, New York 10020

Book design by Angela Carlino
The text of this book is set in New Caledonia.
The illustrations are rendered in colored pencils.

First Edition
Printed in the United States of America
10   9   8   7   6   5

Library of Congress Cataloging-in-Publication Data
Aylesworth, Jim.
Teddy bear tears / by Jim Aylesworth ;
illustrated by Jo Ellen McAllister-Stammen.
p.   cm.
Summary: Each of four beloved teddy bears fears something
at bedtime, and as the little master explains away each fear,
he makes the nighttime worry-free for himself, too.
ISBN 0-689-31776-X
[1. Teddy bears—Fiction. 2. Bedtime—Fiction. 3. Fear of the dark—Fiction.]
I. McAllister-Stammen, Jo Ellen, ill. II. Title.
PZ7.A983Te   1997
[E]—dc20   95-44858

To Mr. Hatch and all of his young friends, with love!
—J. A.

For Mom and Dad, bright lights in the darkness.
—J. S.

There once was a boy
who had four teddy bears.
Their names were Willie
Bear, Fuzzy, Ringo, and
Little Sam.

The little boy loved them all very much, and every night they slept together in a big, cozy bed.

And some nights, there were tears.

They began as soon as the lights went out . . . quiet sniffles. . . .

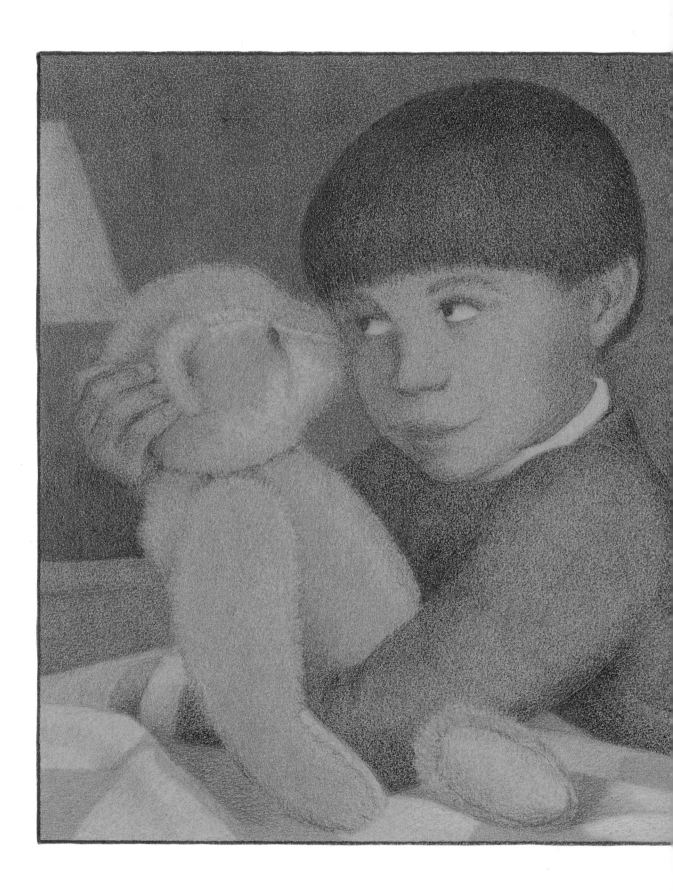

And on this night, they came again.

"Is that you, Willie Bear?" asked the boy as he took Willie Bear into his arms. "Are you crying?"

Willie Bear stopped his sniffling, and with his head up close to the little boy's ear, he whispered in a way that only the little boy could hear. "I heard a scary noise outside the window."

"Don't be scared," said the little boy, getting out of bed and carrying Willie Bear to the window. "See how pretty it is out there in the moonlight? See how the stars shine and how the wind moves the trees?"

Willie Bear nodded.

"Well, that wind makes a noise, but it's nothing to be scared of.

"And sometimes there's a cat out poking around, or maybe a moth bumping against the screen. They make noises, too, but there's nothing out there that would hurt a little bear."

Willie Bear whispered into the little boy's ear. "Okay, but can I sleep up real close to you just in case I hear something else and get scared?"

"Sure," said the little boy. Then he took Willie Bear back to bed, tucked him up real close to his side, and put his arm around him.

For a moment, all was quiet. Then, little sniffles came again.

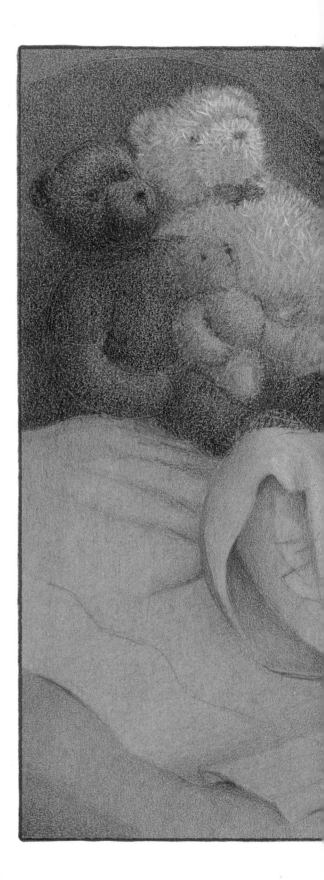

"Is that you, Fuzzy?" The little boy took Fuzzy into his arms and hugged him real close.

Fuzzy stopped his sniffles, and like Willie Bear, he whispered in a way that only the boy could hear. "I'm scared there's something under the bed. Something like an alligator or a cobra or something like that."

"Don't be scared," said
the little boy as he turned
on the lamp and got down
on the floor with Fuzzy in
his arms.

"There's nothing under
here . . . nothing to be
scared of, I mean . . . just
an old sock, a piece from
one of my puzzles, and lots
of dust and stuff. You're not
scared of dust, are you?"

"No," whispered Fuzzy.
"But just in case, can I sleep
up close to you and Willie
Bear? I'd feel much better
if I did."

The little boy got back
into bed and turned out the
light.

He tucked Willie Bear up
real close on one side and
Fuzzy up real close on the
other side, and put his arms
around them both.

And for a moment, there
wasn't a sound.

Then the little sniffles
came again.

"Ringo? You too?" He pulled Ringo up into his arms and hugged him tight.

Ringo's furry head was right up next to the boy's ear, and very softly, he whispered, "There's a bogey man in the closet."

"Ringo, you know there is no such thing as a bogey man!" said the little boy, turning on the lamp again and taking Ringo over to the closet.

"And there's nothing in this closet that could hurt you! Just my clothes and shoes and stuff." Then he turned on the closet light so Ringo could get a better look. "Do you see anything scary in here?"

"No," answered Ringo. "But could I sleep up close to you and Willie Bear and Fuzzy anyway? Just in case?"

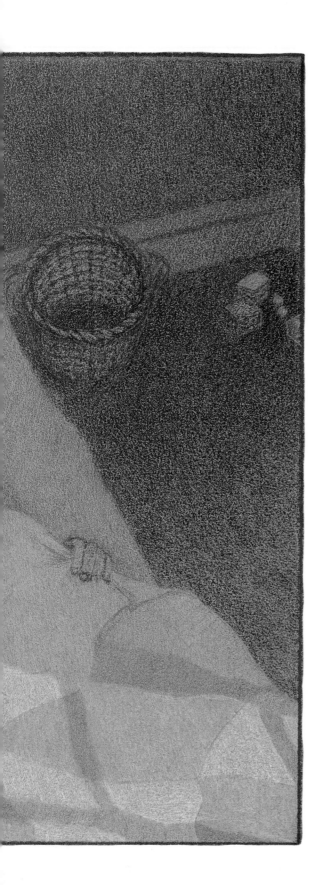

The little boy climbed back in bed.

He tucked Willie Bear up real close on one side, and Fuzzy up real close on the other side, and he put Ringo up on top. Then, he put his arms around all three and closed his eyes.

But right away, more sniffles started.

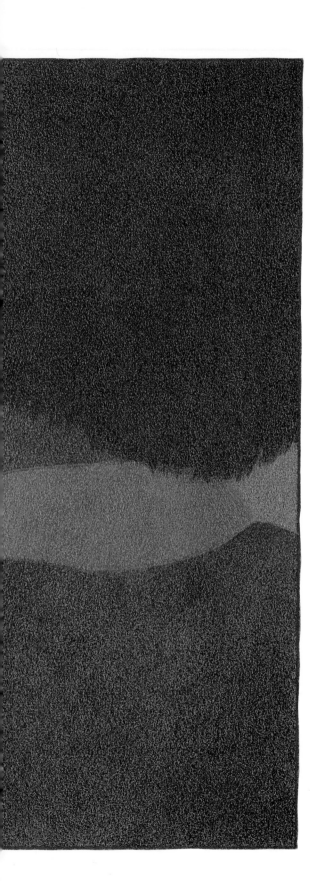

"That has to be you, Little
Sam," said the boy.

He reached for Little
Sam and hugged him close.

Little Sam whispered into
the boy's ear. "It's too dark
in here. It scares me to be
so dark."

"Oh, Little Sam," said the boy. "There's no reason to be afraid of the dark." He got out of bed, ran across the hall, and flipped on the bathroom light.

When he returned, there was a patch of soft light lying across the end of the bed. "Is that better now?" asked the little boy.

"Yes," whispered Sam. "But can't I sleep up close with you and Willie Bear and Fuzzy and Ringo? Just in case?"

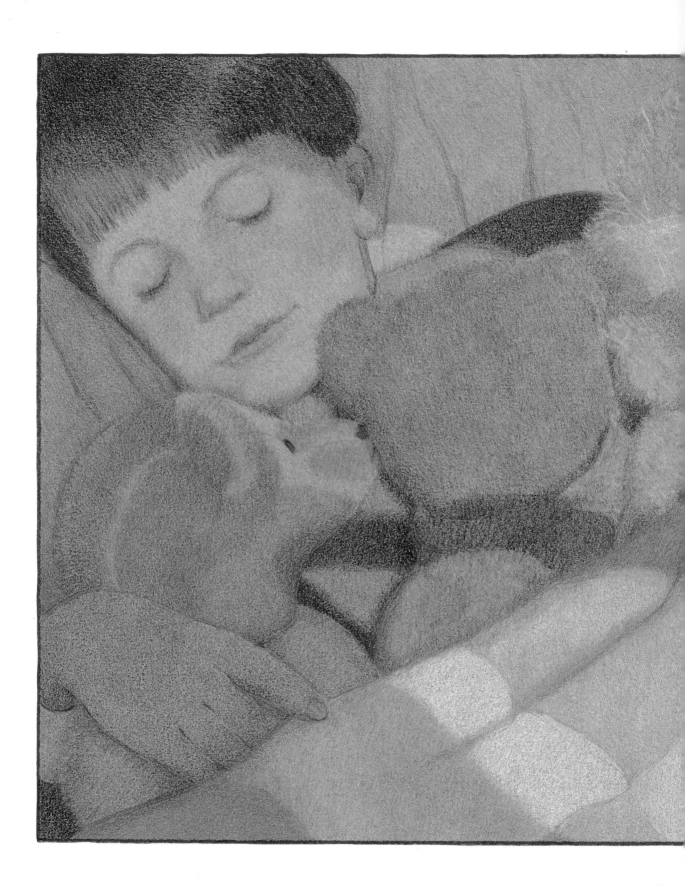

"Sure," said the little boy, and he settled back down on his pillow. He tucked Willie Bear up real close on one side and Fuzzy up real close on the other side. Ringo and Little Sam he put up on top. Then he put his arms around them all.

"Good night, you guys," said the little boy. "I love you."

"We love you, too," said the bears.

And then, after only a moment more, the boy was sound asleep . . .

. . . and dreaming very pleasant dreams.